Chapter books from
Henry Holt and Company

Boo's Dinosaur
Betsy Byars, illustrated by Erik Brooks

Dragon Tooth Trouble
written and illustrated by Sarah Wilson

Fat Bat and Swoop
written and illustrated by Leo Landry

Lavender
Karen Hesse, illustrated by Andrew Glass

Little Horse
Betsy Byars, illustrated by David McPhail

Little Horse on His Own
Betsy Byars, illustrated by David McPhail

Little Raccoon
Lilian Moore, illustrated by Doug Cushman

Sable
Karen Hesse, illustrated by Marcia Sewall

Sea Surprise
written and illustrated by Leo Landry

The Secret Lunch Special (Second-Grade Friends, Book I)
Peter Catalanotto and Pamela Schembri,
illustrated by Peter Catalanotto

Dragon Tooth Trouble

Dragon Tooth Trouble

Sarah Wilson

Henry Holt and Company
New York

Henry Holt and Company, LLC
Publishers since 1866
175 Fifth Avenue
New York, New York 10010
www.henryholtchildrensbooks.com

Henry Holt® is a registered trademark of Henry Holt and Company, LLC.
Distributed in Canada by H. B. Fenn and Company Ltd.

Library of Congress Cataloging-in-Publication Data
Wilson, Sarah.
Dragon tooth trouble / Sarah Wilson.—1st ed.
p.   cm.
Summary: Everyone is in for a hot time when Zoey and her
three dragon friends visit Dr. Frumble the singing dentist.
ISBN-13: 978-0-8050-7830-5 / ISBN-10: 0-8050-7830-4
[1. Dental care—Fiction. 2. Dragons—Fiction.] I. Title.
PZ7.W6986Dra 2006   [E]—dc22   2006001670

First Edition—2006 / Designed by Amelia May Anderson
Printed in the United States of America on acid-free paper. ∞

1 3 5 7 9 10 8 6 4 2

For Miss Christadoro wherever she may be,

still making music for young dragons

Contents

1

A Morning Skip

Zoey and Ginger were out for a morning skip with Ginger's brothers when Ginger began to slow down.

Slowing down was fine with Zoey.

Ginger was a dragon and so were her brothers, Ben and Buster. Zoey was a girl. It was hard for her to keep up with them.

Suddenly, Ginger opened her mouth and howled. Showers of red-hot sparks shot out.

"Ouch!" yelled Buster. "You almost lit my tail!"

"Sorry," Ginger shrugged. "I can't help it. I'm upset!"

"What's wrong, pardner?" asked Ben. Ben and Buster liked to pretend they were cowboys. They called themselves the Buckley Boys.

SPLUNK! Ginger plopped down on the grass and put her head in her claws.

"I have a loose tooth," she rumbled. "It won't stay in, and it won't fall out! It hurts!"

"Wow!" Zoey said. "I'd better get the bubble gum. Chewing might help."

"*Lots* of bubble gum, I reckon!" drawled Ben.

"Extra strength!" added Buster.

"Grape, please," Ginger told Zoey, "but bring it FAST—before this tooth *really* fires up!"

2

Purple Smoke and Fireballs

Pop! Bang! Zoey's bubble gum made things worse.

Ginger chewed and popped gum bubbles, but her tooth wouldn't budge. Instead, purple smoke began to billow out of her mouth. So did purple sparks and fireballs. They smelled like grapes.

"Oooooh!" cried Zoey.
"FIREWORKS!" cheered Ben and Buster.
"OWWWW!" moaned Ginger.

"Sorry," Zoey said. "Don't worry. We can tie a rope around that tooth and yank it out."

"We don't have any rope," said Buster.

"Somebody hightailed it with our lassos!" said Ben.

Ginger's face turned pink. "I used your rope to make pot holders," she confessed. "I was going to surprise you."

Zoey rolled up her sleeves. "It doesn't matter," she said. "I can knock that tooth free all by myself."

"NO!" Ginger yelled. "You're my best friend! What if I accidentally bit you? Or toasted you? That would be awful!"

"Ugh—yes, it would," Zoey agreed.
"Then there's only one thing left to do.
Let's go see Dr. Frumble. *He'll* take care of
this!"

"Dr. Frumble, the singing DENTIST?"
Ginger boomed. "NEVER!"

3

Polka Dots

"Don't you ever go to see Dr. Frumble?"
asked Zoey.

"Never, never, NEVER!" Ginger
repeated. "All that singing! All that tooth
poking! My brothers are the ones who
should see Dr. Frumble! Their volcano
breath is AWFUL."

Ben and Buster clamped their mouths
shut and covered them with their claws.

Zoey pretended not to see.

"Come *on*," she urged Ginger. "It'll be
fine."

"We'll put on our spurs and go with you," offered Ben and Buster.

"Leave me ALONE!" Ginger protested.

In the end, it took all three of them to push her to Dr. Frumble's outdoor office.

"Go, go, go!" they shouted, shoving her forward.

Ginger yelled even louder. "NO, NO, NO!" she bellowed as her tail bumped behind her. *Whomph! Whomph! Whomph!*

They made so much noise that Dr. Frumble and Nurse Sally ran over to meet them.

"Aha!" Dr. Frumble said through the dragon smoke. "Tooth trouble? Open up and let's have a look!"

At that, Ginger broke out in orange polka dots . . . and fainted.

4

Tooth Work

Right away, Dr. Frumble began to sing.

Singing made him relax. He thought it made his patients relax, too. And because he was a nice man, no one wanted to tell him how terrible he sounded.

Ben and Buster propped Ginger against a tree and covered their ears.

Dr. Frumble didn't notice. He went on
singing as he jumped into his fireproof
suit. Then he brought over a stool.

"Nurse Sally is taking tuba lessons.
It's very exciting," he said to Zoey and
the Buckley Boys as he climbed up to face
Ginger. "I've asked her to play a song or
two while I work."

Then he leaned toward Ginger's mouth with his tooth-puller. "Tra-la-la-LA!" he sang.

"OOOOoooooof-ulp," Ginger snorted with her eyes still closed.

Bar-rumph! Bar-rumph! boomed the tuba. *Bar-rumph!* Even Nurse Sally looked surprised at the fuss her music was making.

But Dr. Frumble liked the tuba sounds.
He sang even louder. This was the way
he worked best.

5

Bingo!

Finally Dr. Frumble shouted, "Bingo!"

He was still wearing his helmet, so his voice was muffled.

"Look!" Dr. Frumble said. He held up Ginger's tooth for everybody to see. "Not much smoke, not much fire. This was really a snap!"

"Wow!" said Nurse Sally.

"Ooooof!" Ginger huffed as she woke up. "Why are my ears ringing?"

"Forget your ears," Zoey said. "Feel where your loose tooth was!"

Ginger frowned and wiggled her tongue.

"It doesn't hurt anymore!" she said.

Then she yawned out a few purple sparks and smiled. Not a small smile, either. A horn-to-horn, nose-lighting dragon smile!

"Yahoo!" cheered Zoey. "I'm so glad this tooth stuff is over!"

"Not so fast!" warned Dr. Frumble. "There's *more!*"

6

A Quick Recess

"More what?" everybody wanted to know.

"That's it for Ginger," Dr. Frumble explained, unzipping his fireproof suit. "Now I need to talk to Ben and Buster! Wait while I find my mirror."

After he left, Nurse Sally wrapped up Ginger's tooth in flowered paper and tied a big bow on top.

"For the dragon tooth fairy," she said. "I love making bows. I wish I could do this all the time."

"We do, too," said Zoey.

The Buckley Boys weren't much for bows or tooth fairies. They didn't know what to do next, so they stomped around and blew soot out of the office.

When the cleanup was finished, they
sent their sister a windy kiss—*WHOOOSH!*

They were both glad the visit was over.
"We'll hit the trail now," said Ben with
a twang.

"See you back at the ranch!" said Buster, straightening his neckerchief.

"NO, NO, NO!" Dr. Frumble cried as he wheeled up a dragon-proof mirror. "I have something important to show you two!"

31

7

Moss-Covered Rocks

The "something important" was in
Dr. Frumble's mirror.

"Take a look at *your* mouths, Ben and
Buster," he said, nudging them forward.

"Eeeek!" yelped Ben.

"Ack!" squeaked Buster.

Dr. Frumble nodded. "Those teeth look
like old moss-covered rocks," he said.

"Too many gravel snacks and yummy
campfires, I'll bet."

"Well . . . " The Buckley Boys rolled
their eyes.

"Don't you two *ever* brush or look in
mirrors?" Zoey wondered.

"We only see ourselves when we fly over lakes," allowed Ben. "Mirrors steam up on us."

"Or we accidentally set them on fire," admitted Buster.

"Nurse Sally and I will fix things," soothed Dr. Frumble. "Just a few songs and one good scrubbing and those teeth will be like new!"

"NOW?" gulped the Buckley Boys.

"Yes, and not a minute too soon," said Dr. Frumble.

"Uh-oh," muttered Ben.

"We'll come back some other time," mumbled Buster. "Bye, Sis. Bye, Zoey."

The Buckley Brothers flapped their
wings to make a fast retreat, but—
CLOMPH!—Ginger stood on their tails.
"Not so fast!" she said.

8

Fireballs, Again

The Buckley Boys wiggled and squirmed.

Dr. Frumble sang as he zipped up his fireproof suit again and brought out his brushes.

"This will be easy, boys," he told them. "Why don't we ask Nurse Sally to play her tuba once more?"

Ben and Buster's faces turned blue, orange, pink, and purple.

"Sister cowgirl, let us GO!" Ben pleaded. "It's not fair! When it was your turn, you fainted!"

"And you didn't wake up until your loose tooth was out," added Buster.

"True," said Ginger. "But *I* don't have volcano breath! Besides, cowboys do what needs to be done."

The Buckley Boys opened their mouths
to say more, but—*KA-BOOM! KA-BOOM!*—
instead of words, fireballs burst out of
their mouths. Fireballs that whizzed
around Dr. Frumble's office—*zap-zap-zap!*

Swooosh! Thick smoke clouds rolled
through the office, too.

"STOP that right now!" ordered Ginger.

"We can't help it!" Ben and Buster roared back.

"Uh-oh," said Zoey.

9

More Tooth Work

"They really *can't* help it," Ginger told
Dr. Frumble. "When our family gets upset
we shoot back fireballs. It's just our way."

Zoey agreed. "Dragons are really very
sensitive," she said.

"That's for sure!" exclaimed Dr. Frumble.
Then a strange look crossed his face. "My
shoes are melting!"

"Oh my," said Nurse Sally. "I've never seen shoes melt before."

"Can I see?" asked Ben squinting down at Dr. Frumble.

"Me, too," said Buster.

"HURRY," interrupted Dr. Frumble. "Nurse Sally, run for the fire extinguisher. If these fireballs melted my shoes, they might melt ALL of us!"

Nurse Sally dashed off and came back with something she thought was a fire extinguisher. But the smoke was so thick she couldn't see. And no one could see her, either. "Here it comes!" she yelled. "I'll make big foam bows! Yippee!"

10

Sploot!

Dr. Frumble shook off his shoes. He was still jumping.

Nurse Sally aimed the fire extinguisher and shot foamy bows in all directions.

Just in time, too.

SPLOOT! went the foam. *FIZZZzzzz!* went the fireballs. *Poof!* went the dragon smoke.

In just a few seconds, everyone—even Dr. Frumble—was mint green and covered in sticky, pasty goo.

"I can't believe it!" he said in surprise. "Nurse Sally, this isn't fire foam at all. It's my new invention—Shake-and-Shoot Dragon Toothpaste!"

"Oops!" said Nurse Sally.

"You mean this squishy stuff is *toothpaste*?" cried Zoey. "It tastes like mint jelly."

"Whatever it is, I like it," Ginger said. "It's polished up my scales."

"It's polished EVERYTHING!" shouted Dr. Frumble, still wide-eyed. "My watch is shiny! Our faces are clean! And, Buckley Boys, you must have kept your mouths open, because—guess what?—your teeth are WHITE!"

"WHAA-HOO!" whooped Ben and Buster.

"What a GREAT Tooth Day!" cheered Zoey.

11

An Afternoon Dip

The whole group half-ran, half-flew to a nearby lake to wash off the minty goo.

While they were splashing, they admired the new gap in Ginger's smile.

"Lovely!" said Nurse Sally.

"It IS special, isn't it?" said Ginger, beaming.

"Perfect for bubble-gum blowing," said Zoey.

"For water-spitting, too!" said Ben and Buster.

It was also a great day for the Buckley Boys. They could actually see their faces in each other's shiny clean teeth.

"Brilliant!" they told each other.

But Dr. Frumble was the happiest of all.
"This is WONDERFUL!" he said. "I can't
get over it. I won't have to climb in your
mouths to clean teeth anymore. I'll just
use my Shake-and-Shoot Toothpaste
foam!"

"It'll dazzle up the rest of us, too," said Ginger. "We need to CELEBRATE!"

"We sure do," said Zoey.

So Ginger and her brothers spread out their wings to make boat oars. "Come on!" they said as the others climbed on their backs. Then they paddled all around the lake, showing their toothy grins and singing until supper time.

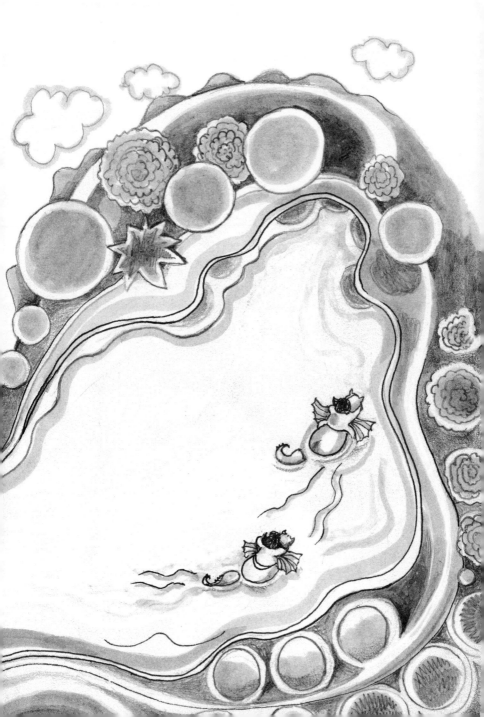